Storyteller Tales

The Littlest Camel
and other Christmas stories

All around the world people celebrate
Christmas in different ways, often
continuing traditions that began centuries
ago. Here is a selection of stories – some
old and some new – showing how some
popular Christmas customs began.

Bob Hartman is a widely acclaimed
author and storyteller. He is best known
for *The Lion Storyteller Bible* and other books
in the *Storyteller* series in which these tales
were originally published.

Other titles in this series

The Noisy Stable

The Crocodile Brother

The Generous Rabbit

Polly and the Frog

Why Dogs Chase Cats

The Littlest Camel

and other Christmas stories

Bob Hartman

Illustrations by
Brett Hudson

LION
CHILDREN'S

A Lion Children's Book
an imprint of
Lion Hudson plc
Mayfield House, 256 Banbury Road,
Oxford OX2 7DH, England
www.lionhudson.com
ISBN 0 7459 4825 1

First edition 2004
10 9 8 7 6 5 4 3 2 1 0

Acknowledgments
These stories were first published in
The Lion Storyteller Christmas Book

A catalogue record for this book is available
from the British Library

Typeset in 15/23 Baskerville MT Schlbk
Printed and bound in Great Britain by Cox and
Wyman Ltd, Reading

Contents

The Little Lambs   7
A Story from Arabia

The Raven   15
A Story from France

The Littlest Camel   21
A Story from Syria

Old Befana   28
A Story from Italy

The Icicles   37
A Traditional Folk Tale

The First Christmas Tree   42
A Story from Germany

Francis' Christmas Pageant   48
A Story from Italy

The First Tinsel 52
A Story from the Ukraine

A Flower for Christmas 59
A Story from Sweden

The Little Lambs

Once upon a time, there were two little lambs. They lived with their flock on a hill outside Bethlehem. And every night, before they fell asleep, they would sit around the fire and listen to the tales of a wise, old shepherd.

Some of the stories were exciting, and the little lambs could hardly get to sleep.

Some tales were funny, and the little

lambs would roll with laughter.

Others were scary, and the little lambs would snuggle extra close to their mother sheep.

But one night, the old shepherd told a special tale – a story about something that was yet to happen.

'One day,' he said slowly, 'one day, a king

will be born. He will be powerful. He will be good. And he will put right what is wrong in this world. But here is the amazing thing!

He will not be born in a palace. He will not be born to the rich and the mighty. No – he will be born to poor and ordinary people. People just like us!'

The two little lambs had never heard such a thing.

'A king!' said the first.

'A king and a shepherd!' said the second.

And secretly, they both wondered the same thing: Where is this king? And when can we go and see him?

One crisp, clear night, a few weeks later, the old shepherd told the story again. And when he had finished, one lamb turned to the other.

'I want to see this king!' he whispered.

'Me too!' said the second little lamb.

'Why don't we try to find him – tonight!'

And so they pretended to go to sleep.

They shut their eyes. They baa-ed and they snuffled and they snored. And when their mother sheep was finally fast asleep, they sneaked out of the sheepfold and hurried down the hill.

They peeped into the shepherds' huts first. No baby there.

Then they crept around every dimming campfire. No king there, either.

'What now?' asked the first lamb.

The second lamb thought for a minute. And then he said just one word: 'Grass.'

'Grass?' asked the first lamb.

'Yes,' nodded the second. 'When we are

looking for grass, we go from hill to hill, don't we? And the shepherd never stops until he finds the greenest pasture. That's what we'll do. We'll never stop, until we find the king!'

And so they searched – from hill to hill and valley to valley, halfway through that dark night. But still they found no baby king.

At last, they came to a road.

'I'm tired,' said the first lamb. 'I want to go home!'

'But here is a road!' said the second lamb. 'Maybe it will take us to the king!'

'You go if you want to,' the first lamb sighed. 'I'm going back.' And that's just what he did.

But the second little lamb would not give up. So he started down that road.

It was dark and it was late and he was frightened. So the little lamb tried hard to remember the old shepherd's funny stories. And he tried even harder to forget the scary ones!

Suddenly, the sky turned bright. Behind him, over the hills, there was light and – could it be? – singing! And ahead of him, the sky seemed brighter too. For a star shone high in the heavens, lighting up a little town below.

The little lamb started to run. Something special was happening, and he wanted to see it, even if it had nothing to do with that special king.

He followed the star to a stable. And there, among the sleepy beasts, were a mother and a father and a baby.

The lamb crept in and nuzzled the child. The child patted the lamb on his woolly head. And it wasn't long before the shepherds, and their sheep – and his tired brother too – came creeping in as well.

'What are you doing here?' asked the old
shepherd, when he spotted the little lamb.
'I know. You're here to see the king I told
you about.' Then he pointed at the baby.
'Well, there he is. A good king. A powerful
king. A king who will, one day, put right
what is wrong with this world. A king born
poor and ordinary – just like us!'

The Raven

Raven was a jealous bird.

He was jealous of Robin and Bluebird and Dove, for they were more beautiful than him.

And he was jealous of Sparrow and Nightingale too, for he could never hope to sing like them.

So Raven flew through the night skies, a sad and bitter shadow, calling out his lonely caw-caw.

One cold December night, Raven sensed
suddenly that he was not alone. He felt the
sky above him shiver, as if he were in the
wake of some much larger bird – Eagle,
perhaps, or Vulture. But then Raven heard
singing too – singing so lovely that it could
never have come from the throats of those
two high-flying hunters.

Jealousy struck Raven first. Why should
he bother with yet another bird and its
golden voice? But curiosity was there as well.
And so, fighting his jealousy, Raven looked
up into the sky. And there, floating above
him, were no birds at all, but a flock of
golden angels!

'Good news!' the angels sang. 'We have
good news! God's own Son is born in
Bethlehem tonight! And you, Raven, must

go and tell all the other birds!'

'Me?' Raven croaked. 'Why me? I am
the ugliest of the birds, and as for my voice –
well, you can hear for yourselves! They will
never listen to me.'

'But you have been chosen,' the angels sang. And, without another word, they flew off into the night.

What could Raven do? The birds had to know. And he, of all birds, had been chosen to tell them. And so he flew down from the sky, down to the tree tops – his cry as sharp and piercing as the winter night.

'Christ is born!' he called – called to Robin and to Bluebird and to Dove. 'Born in Bethlehem tonight!'

'Then we must go and see him,' they chirped. And Raven was surprised, for not one of them mentioned how ugly Raven was.

'Christ is born!' he called again – called to Sparrow and to Nightingale.

'Then we must go and sing to him!' they twittered. And again Raven was surprised,

for not one of them said a thing about the
harshness of Raven's voice.

And so Raven flew to Bethlehem too.

He watched the baby reach out and touch
Robin's red breast. He heard the baby
giggle and coo along with Nightingale's
sweet lullaby. And he wished that he could
do something more than perch high in the
stable's dark rafters.

'But don't you see?' came a voice –
a sweet sing-song voice amid the flutter of
golden wings. 'You have done the most
important thing of all. For none of the other
birds would be here, if you had not pierced
the night with your cries and told them the
good news.'

Then the angel disappeared. And leaving
his jealousy behind, Raven took flight too –
down from the rafters to join the others at
the side of the child.

The Littlest Camel

'Hurry along!' snorted the Big Brown Camel
from the back of the caravan. 'Hurry along,
or we'll never catch up!'

'He's going as fast as he can!' said Mother
Camel. 'You can't ask for more than that.'

And the Littlest Camel? The Littlest
Camel said nothing. For it was all he could
do to keep his little legs moving.

Up the sand dunes and down the sand

dunes. Over the mountains and across the
rocky plains.

He had done nothing but walk for weeks.
And when the walking was over, he would
sleep – fast and deep – snuggled at his
mother's side.

'He shouldn't even be here!' grunted the
Big Brown Camel. And he spat on the dusty
track. 'He's not big enough to carry
anything. And he's slow. Much too slow!'

'But it's not his fault!' said Mother Camel.
'How many times do I have to tell you? The

camel driver made a mistake. He picked me
out at the market – just where he bought
you – but he didn't see my baby beside me.
And by the time we reached the desert and
he noticed, it was too late to turn back.'

'Well, I'm not going to get left behind.
I promise you that!' the Big Brown Camel
grunted.

Again, the Littlest Camel didn't say a
word. He just tried to keep his legs moving.
One, two, three, four. One, two, three, four.

And that's when somebody shouted, 'The

star has stopped! Look, there's the town.'

'It won't be long now, dear,' said Mother Camel. And the Littlest Camel smiled. He couldn't wait to rest his weary legs. But as they entered the town, everyone started to speed up, for the men at the front of the caravan were anxious to reach their destination.

Maybe that's why it happened. Or perhaps it was because the Big Brown Camel was in such a hurry. But when they turned a corner in one of Bethlehem's narrow streets, the Littlest Camel tripped and fell tumbling to the ground.

The Big Brown Camel stepped right over him. 'I'm not waiting for you!' he grunted.

And even though Mother Camel turned and tried to stop, the camel driver was in

such a rush that he whipped her back into
the line.

The Littlest Camel picked himself up, leg
by bony leg. Then he ran as fast as those
legs would carry him, after his mother and
the rest of the caravan. Through the streets
he followed them, always just that bit too far
behind.

But when they finally stopped – beasts
and men alike, falling on their knees before

a simple stable – the Littlest Camel could not slow down! And so he tripped and tumbled one more time –past camels and servants and three men with bright gifts – and landed head-first at the foot of a wooden manger.

The Littlest Camel shook his head.

The Littlest Camel opened his eyes.

The Littlest Camel was face-to-face with a little baby!

The baby smiled at him and patted his camel nose.

And that's when the camel heard these words: 'Well done, little camel. You travelled far to see my Son. And you never gave up. So from now on, it will be a camel, the Littlest Camel, who will bring gifts to the children of this land.'

And that is why, to this day, children in the Middle East receive their Christmas gifts from the back of a camel – a little camel, just like the one who brought joy to the child in the manger.

Old Befana

Shoop, shoop, shoop. Old Befana swept the floor.

Shoop, shoop, shoop. She swept out the cupboards too.

Shoop, shoop, shoop. Old Befana swept up every bit of dirt, every tumbling dustball and every little crumb.

Old Befana's house was spotless! And her front step too. And the path that led to the road.

Sweeping was all that Old Befana did. It was all that Old Befana loved. And so she was annoyed when, early one morning, in the midst of her sweeping, she was disturbed by a loud Bang, Bang, Bang! on the door.

She opened the door, the broom still in her hand. And she was greeted by three tall, tired strangers.

'We have travelled all night,' said the first stranger.

'We are following a star,' explained the second.

'And we need somewhere to sleep,' begged the third.

Old Befana looked at the three men. They were very well dressed. There were jewels on their hats and on their gowns and on the chains that hung round their necks. They

could have been rich merchants, or wizards, or kings. In any case, they did not look like robbers. And as for her sweeping – well, the bedroom had already been swept for the day. So she nodded her head and welcomed them in.

She showed them the way to the bedroom, and when she looked in on them a few minutes later, she discovered that they were all fast asleep in one bed – the covers pulled up tight under their big beards!

Old Befana returned to her sweeping.

Shoop, shoop, shoop. She swept the kitchen.

Shoop, shoop, shoop. She swept the living room too.

Shoop, shoop, shoop. She swept the step and the path to the road.

And all the while she swept, she wondered, 'Where do they come from? Where are they going? And why do they sleep all day?'

So when, at last, the three strangers awoke, she asked them.

'We come from the East,' said the first stranger, 'and have travelled all night.'

'We are following a star,' said the second.

'A star that will lead us to the King of all Kings,' explained the third. 'A king who is but a little child!'

Then the three strangers made Old Befana a most unusual offer.

'Since you have been so kind to us...' began the first stranger.

'And since you have given us a place to rest...' continued the second.

'We would like you to come with us!' invited the third, 'to see this king and to bring him gifts!'

Old Befana was so surprised that she

nearly dropped her broom. What an
adventure! she thought. To follow a star
and find a king!

But then she looked at her broom. And
she looked around her house. And it didn't
take her long to imagine how dusty
everything would be if she ceased her

33

sweeping for even one day.

So she sadly shook her head and said, 'No, thank you.' And the three strangers walked off into the night.

Old Befana went to sleep, but her dreams were interrupted by visions of strangers and stars and kings. The next morning, she picked up her broom, as usual, but try as she might, she could not keep her mind on her sweeping.

Shoop, shoop, shoop. She swept the living room. But all she could think of was the strangers' invitation.

Shoop, shoop. She swept the kitchen. But all she could think of was that wandering star.

Shoop. She swept the front step. But all she could think of was the little king – who was down that road, somewhere, in a house, with a path and a step like hers.

And that's when she decided she would join the strangers after all. So with the broom in one hand, and an apron full of little gifts, she set off down the road.

She walked and she walked. She searched and she searched. But, sadly, Old Befana

never did find the three strangers. And, so they say, she is walking still – with a broom in her hand and with an apron full of gifts. And each Christmas, she walks up every path, climbs up every step and visits every house. And wherever she finds a child, she leaves a little gift. For she never can be certain which of those children is the 'King of all Kings'!

The Icicles

Through the woods they walked – Joseph and Mary and little Jesus.

King Herod was dead. They were safe at last. And so they were going home – all the way from Egypt to Nazareth.

The days were warm enough. Too warm, sometimes. So they would rest, when they could, in some welcoming shadow.

But the nights were cold – especially the

nights in the hills. And this night was the coldest of them all!

The trees looked down on them and shook their leafless branches.

'They'll freeze to death!' said the cedar.

'They must find shelter,' said the birch.

'And look at the little boy,' sighed the pine tree. 'He can hardly keep from shivering.'

'But what can we do?' asked the cedar. 'My branches are bare. The wind will blow right through them.'

'Mine are no better,' nodded the birch.

And then they both looked at the pine tree.

'Of course!' she shouted. 'Why didn't I think of it myself?' And at once, she began to shake her furry boughs – so hard and so strong that Mary and Joseph could not fail to notice her.

'Look!' cried Joseph. 'A pine tree! If we huddle together beneath the branches, perhaps we can keep the wind out, and stay warm through the night.'

Mary agreed.

And little Jesus just shivered. So the three of them crept under the prickly pine boughs and wrapped themselves up in their blankets.

The wind blew and blew. The night grew frosty and sharp. Snowflakes began to fall. But through it all, Joseph and Mary and little Jesus slept safe and warm.

'They're still alive!' said the cedar to the pine tree.

'I think you've saved them!' added the birch.

And then the pine tree heard another voice – the glad song of a passing angel.

'Well done, pine tree!' the angel sang. 'For your warm boughs have sheltered the Son of God, himself!'

The pine tree could hardly believe it.

And in her excitement, she began to weep – tears of happiness, tears of joy! The tears trickled down her bushy branches. And as they trickled, they froze – froze in long, icy strands, all the way down to the ground.

When Mary and Joseph and Jesus awoke the next morning, they crawled out from under the tree. And what they saw made the little boy jump with delight.

'Look!' he called. 'Look at all the pretty icicles.'

And so they were, shining like diamonds in the morning sun.

And perhaps that is why some people still dress their Christmas trees with icicle decoration – in memory of that clever pine tree and her beautiful frozen tears.

The First
Christmas Tree

Boniface was walking through the woods.
It was winter. It was cold. But even though
Boniface was desperate for a hot drink and
a warm fire, he kept on walking. For it was
his job to travel, from one end of England
to the other, telling the people about Jesus.
Boniface heard a cry. It was a child's cry.
A frightened cry. So Boniface stopped
walking and began to run.

The branches snapped at his face. The wind howled about him. But he was getting closer, he could tell, for the child's cries were growing louder.

At last, Boniface stumbled into a clearing. There, gathered at the foot of an oak tree, was a group of men – and the child's cry came from the midst of them.

'Stop!' Boniface shouted. 'Stop what you are doing! Now!'

The men turned towards him. Their faces were painted with strange and frightening patterns and each one held a weapon.

'Go away!' one of them called back. 'This is no business of yours!'

'Yes it is!' Boniface replied. 'For I can tell, by your dress and by your face-paint, that you are Druids. And if I am not mistaken, you intend to kill that boy and offer him as a sacrifice to one of your tree gods.'

'The god of the oak demands it!' one Druid argued. 'And we are here to serve him.'

'Well, I serve another God!' argued Boniface. 'A God who does not approve of the killing of children.' And with that, he grabbed an axe and began to chop at the

base of the oak tree. One of the Druids went to stop him, but the leader held him back.

'Wait,' he said with a sneer. 'The god of the oak tree will punish him soon enough!'

Boniface chopped and chopped. He chopped until he had chopped that oak tree down. And as it crashed to the forest floor, the Druids began to tremble.

'I don't understand,' said their leader.

'The god in the oak tree did nothing to protect himself – and nothing to punish you!'

'That's because there is no god in the tree!' Boniface explained. 'There is only one God – the God who made the tree, and everything else in this world. The God who does not demand the sacrifice of our sons. No, for he has already sacrificed his own Son, Jesus – sacrificed him on a tree – to take away all that is wrong in this world.'

'He sacrificed his own son?' said the Druid leader in wonder.

'Yes,' said Boniface. 'And more amazing than that, he brought his Son back to life again, so that we could live for ever too!'

And then Boniface pointed to a tree. Not the fallen oak, but a bright, furry evergreen.

'If you want to remember the God I

serve,' Boniface said, 'you could use that tree
– the tree that never dies. Decorate it, and
use it to celebrate the birth of Jesus – the Son
of God, who lives for ever!'

So that's what the Druids did. And some
people say that was the very first Christmas
tree!

Francis' Christmas Pageant

The village of Greccio sat on a wooded hill across the valley from Mount Terminillo. On the rocky slopes of that mountain there were caves. And in one of those caves a man named Francis had built a little church.

Francis was a good man, a saint. He rebuilt broken-down churches, helped broken-down people, and travelled across this poor broken-down world talking about the love of God.

One cold Christmas Eve, Francis decided to do something special for the people who lived in Greccio. He called together his friends, a group of monks called the Little Brothers, and he asked them to bring him a wooden manger. He asked for a donkey as well. And a big brown cow. And when he had put them in the cave, he sent out the Little Brothers again.

'Go to the village,' he said. Invite everyone. Tell them there is something special waiting for them in the cave.'

The monks did as they were asked and it wasn't long before Francis could see the villagers streaming up the mountainside: A boy with a stick, a little girl, a baker and blacksmith and a fat old man. A jester and a soldier. A tall man on a horse with a fine lady beside him. A crippled old woman and a beggar and a priest.

They were all there, every one, carrying torches to light their way, so bright against the dark hillside that they could have been stars on that first Christmas night, or the angels who sang to the shepherds.

When they reached the cave, Francis called one woman forward to kneel, like Mary, at the manger's side. Then he asked a man to stand and watch over her, like Joseph. Finally, Francis began to sing. He sang the story of that first Christmas, and the

people of Greccio wept when they heard
how God had chosen a poor woman, poorer
even than themselves to give birth to his own
Son, Jesus.

And so they sang God's praises through
the night – Saint Francis and the people of
Greccio, at the very first Christmas pageant!

The First Tinsel

It was Christmas Eve and, at last, everything was quiet.

The children had finally forced themselves to sleep.

Mother and Father were snoring away, exhausted, in their bed.

And even the mice were snuggled safe in their holes.

So that's when the spiders came out –

crawling through the crack in the corner of
the ceiling.

'The coast is clear!' called Mr Spider.

'I'm coming as fast as I can!' called his
wife in return.

It was the same every night. They would
anchor two long, sticky strands to the ceiling,
and swing across the room, down to the floor
on the other side. Then they would snip the
silky strands and explore! Up and down the
curtains they would go, over and under each
chair. And if, along the way, they happened
to stumble across a wandering fly or a
wayward ant, then they would enjoy a
midnight snack as well!

'Hang on tight!' said Mr Spider.

'Eight legs' worth!' said Mrs Spider in return.

And with a leap and a 'Yahoo!' the

spiders sailed across the room.

They should have reached the far end of the room, just as normal. But it was Christmas Eve, remember? So instead of landing on the floor, they crashed into something tall and prickly!

'It's a tree!' called Mr Spider. 'I'm pretty sure it's a tree!'

'But it wasn't here last night,' wondered Mrs Spider. 'How did it grow so fast?'

'Perhaps we should explore it,' suggested Mr Spider.

'Excellent!' Mrs Spider agreed. And then, licking her lips, she added, 'I hear that grubs live in trees, and I haven't eaten a grub in a long time!'

So the spiders crawled down the tree. They started from the star at the top.

Mr Spider went one way.
Mrs Spider went the other.
And they were both so excited
that they forgot about snipping
off the long strands of web that
trailed behind them.

'Look, here's an orange!'
called Mr Spider.

'And an apple!' replied his
wife.

There were pine cones and
candles and bows and bells as
well – it was a tree full of
surprises! But suddenly, just as
they reached the bottom, the
lights in the room flickered
on. So Mr and Mrs Spider did
what any sensible spiders would

– they skittered far under the tree and into the darkest shadow they could find.

At first, they could see only boots. Big black boots with white fur around the tops. Then there were hands. White-gloved hands thrusting huge bright boxes right in front of their spider faces. Then there was chuckling – and the odd, deep 'Ho-ho-ho!' And finally, from that same deep voice, there boomed a 'What's this?'

The man with the black boots and the white gloves stood back and looked at the tree. And then he laughed again – another 'Ho-ho-ho!'

'A spider's been here,' he chuckled. 'And left its web all up and down and around this tree. It's a lovely decoration. It just needs… yes, that's it.'

And he touched the web with the tip of his white-gloved hand.

All at once, the web turned to silver, from the point where he touched it and all around the tree!

When the man had gone and it was dark again, the spiders crawled out from their hiding place. They looked up at the tree,

and at their web, now glistening like silver.

'It's beautiful!' said Mr Spider.

'A wonder!' said Mrs Spider in return.

And some say that's how the very first tinsel came to be!

A Flower for Christmas

Everyone was walking to the church.
Everyone in the little Mexican town. Their
arms were heavy with gifts – fruit and
vegetables and sweets – for it was Christmas
Eve and everyone was expected to bring a
present for the Christ Child.

Manuel watched them all walk by. He
watched them laugh. He watched them
sing. He watched the way they shared their

excitement and joy.

But all he could do was to wipe the tears from his dirty face, for Manuel was a child of the streets – a poor orphan boy with nothing at all to bring.

He had tried begging for something, but the people had only laughed. 'You say you want it for the Christ Child?' they sneered. 'We know your kind. You'll just keep it for yourself!'

He had thought about stealing something too. But stealing? For the Christ Child? Surely that would be worse than bringing no gift at all.

And so he kept his distance. And when the crowd had shuffled into the church, and when the doors had been shut behind them, he crept to an open window and peered in.

Everything was so beautiful – the candles, the decorations and the gifts! There were hundreds of them, piled up round the statue of the Christ Child and his mother.

But the longer Manuel looked, the sadder he felt, until finally, he fell to his knees and he prayed, 'Dear Christ Child, I am not like the people in the church. I have nothing to bring to you this Christmas Eve. So please accept my prayer. And my tears as well.

For they are all I have to give you.'

Manuel wiped his face dry again. Then he opened his eyes. And there, where his tears had fallen, was a flower. A flower that had not been there before. Gold as the star that shone over Bethlehem, that's how bright the flower was. And surrounding it, there were leaves as red as blood!

'It's a miracle!' Manuel cried. And he scooped up the flower, roots and all, and ran into the church.

'Look!' he shouted, running down the aisle. 'Look! I have a gift for the Christ Child too!'

Some people whispered and moaned.

They did not like their service interrupted. But when they saw the flower, their groans turned to sighs of wonder.

'It is a miracle, indeed!' the priest agreed. 'A flower such as I have never seen!'

And so it was that Manuel's poinsettia became known by the special name of 'The Flower of the Holy Night'!

A Note from the Author

As you may wish to read other versions of some of these traditional stories, I would like to acknowledge some of the sources I have referred to, although most of these stories can be found in several collections. You will find the stories listed under the titles used in this book, but they should be easy to identify in the books I mention.

'The Littlest Camel', 'The First Tinsel' and 'The Raven' from *Hark! A Christmas Sampler* by Jane Yolen, G.P. Putnam's Sons, New York, 1991. 'Old Befana', 'The First Christmas Tree', 'The Icicles', 'St Francis' Christmas Pageant' and 'A Flower for Christmas' from *It's Time for Christmas* by Elizabeth Hough Sechrist and Janette Woolsey, Macrae Smith Company, Philadelphia, 1959. 'The Little Lambs' from *Joy to the World* by Ruth Sawyer, Little, Brown and Company, Boston, 1966.